Tiptoe Into Scary Cities

LURID LONDON

by E. Merwin

Consultant: Debbie Felton
Professor of Classics
University of Massachusetts
Amherst, Massachusetts

BEARPORT PUBLISHING

New York, New York

Credits

Cover, © Eric Isselee/Shutterstock, © Valentyna Chuklyebova/Shutterstock, and © Zoltan Gabor/Shutterstock; TOC, © Petar Paunchev/Shutterstock; 4–5, © Nejron Photo/Shutterstock, © Evgeniia Litovchenko/Shutterstock, © Feverstockphoto/iStock, © Bojan Pavlukovic/Shutterstock, © Krivosheev Vitaly/Shutterstock, and © ArtFamily/Shutterstock; 6L, Public Domain; 6R, Public Domain; 7, © DaLiu/iStock; 8L, © tatui suwat/Shutterstock; 8R, © Caters News Agency; 9, © Bridgeman Images; 10–11, © Faezal Omar Baki/Shutterstock, © varandah/Shutterstock, and © Lario Tus/Shutterstock; 12, © Rex/Shutterstock; 13, © wcjohnston/iStock, and © George Marks/iStock; 14L, Public Domain; 14R, © Soundsnaps/Dreamstime and © schankz/Shutterstock; 15, © Lordprice Collection/Alamy; 16, © Ttstudio/Shutterstock; 17, © Alex Segre/Alamy; 17T, © Vasilchenko Nikita/Shutterstock; 18–19, © Ian Grundy; 18, © Laborant/Shutterstock; 19, Public Domain; 20L, © Luuuusa/Shutterstock; 20R, Public Domain; 21, © Bridgeman Images; 23, © chrisdorney/Shutterstock; 24, © Aleksandra H. Kossowska/Shutterstock and © Eric Isselee/Shutterstock.

Publisher: Kenn Goin
Senior Editor: Joyce Tavolacci
Creative Director: Spencer Brinker
Photo Researcher: Thomas Persano
Cover: Kim Jones

Library of Congress Cataloging-in Publication Data in process at time of publication (2019)
Library of Congress Control Number: 2018009288
ISBN-13: 978-1-68402-670-8 (library binding)

For more information, write to Bearport Publishing Company, Inc., 45 West 21st Street, Suite 3B, New York, New York 10010. Printed in the United States of America.

10 9 8 7 6 5 4 3 2 1

CONTENTS

Lurid London

Down a dark and empty London street, your footsteps echo. But you are not alone. Ghostly figures appear. They moan in hushed voices. Some let out piercing cries. They want to know what brings you to their city.

Get ready to read four frightening tales about **lurid** London. Turn the page . . . if you dare.

Phantom Brothers

The Tower of London

A castle with a creepy secret **looms** over London. In 1483, twelve-year-old Prince Edward V was next in line to become king. However, his uncle, Richard III, had other plans.

Richard III

Prince Edward (right) and his brother

The Tower of London was once a prison.

Richard III sent Edward and his brother to the Tower of London.

That's where both young princes disappeared. Then their uncle became king of England.

Fast-forward 200 years. Two small skeletons were found buried near the tower. People say that the bones belonged to the young princes.

Since then, two ghosts have been spotted nearby. Sometimes, they cling to each other out of fear.

In 2017, a visitor snapped a spooky photo of two children. Are they the long-dead princes?

The visitor's creepy photo

The Tower of London was used as a prison for almost 1,000 years. Nearly 100 prisoners were **beheaded** there by axe.

Terror in the Tube

London Underground

Cries can be heard in London's tube, or **subway.** A ghostly girl weeps near the train tracks. Another spirit has long hair and no face. She floats over a spot where ten people were once killed in a train wreck.

Some of London's trains are haunted, too. Long ago, a man boarding a train was crushed to death. Is his spirit trapped? **Conductors** hear footsteps and knocking sounds in empty cars. *Clunk-click, clunk-click*. Doors open and shut mysteriously . . . as if a ghost were controlling them!

The London Underground has 249 miles (401 km) of tunnels all over the city. Many were built on top of **plague pits**.

Ghost Chicken

Highgate

It was a cold, snowy day in 1625. A scientist named Francis Bacon was riding though Highgate in north London. He was thinking about how to use ice to keep food from rotting. Suddenly, he had an idea! He bought a chicken and killed it on the spot. He then stuffed it with snow.

The scientist Francis Bacon

A print showing the Highgate neighborhood in north London

Francis never learned the result of his **experiment.** On his way home, he felt sick. Three days later, he died.

In Highgate, a chicken has been seen running in circles. It's thought to be the ghost of Francis's dead bird. Whenever someone approaches, the chicken **vanishes** into thin air!

The cemetery in Highgate is believed to be a hangout for vampires!

Stage Fright

Drury Lane Theatre

The Drury Lane Theatre puts on some great shows—starring ghosts. In 1735, two men argued over a wig. One of the actors, Charles Macklin, became **livid.** Using a cane, he beat his fellow actor to death.

Since Charles's own death, people say his ghost appears to other actors. His spirit is said to roam the theater—and pass through walls!

The actor Charles Macklin

Another restless spirit is a **zany** clown named Joseph Grimaldi. Joseph shared a weird wish before he died in 1837. He wanted his head to be removed—and this was done! Since that time, the head has been seen floating around the theater.

In 1848, a skeleton was found behind one of the theater's walls. Between its ribs lay a dagger!

Joseph Grimaldi

Joseph Grimaldi as "Joey" the clown

Spooky Spots in London

Glossary

beheaded (bee-HEHD-id) had one's head cut off

conductors (kuhn-DUHK-turz) people who work on trains

experiment (ek-SPAIR-uh-ment) a scientific test set up to find the answer to a question

livid (LIHV-id) very angry

looms (LOOMZ) comes into view

lurid (LUHR-id) shocking and disturbing

plague pits (PLAYG PIHTS) huge holes where the bodies of people who died from a deadly disease were buried

subway (SUHB-way) an underground electric railroad

vanishes (VAN-ish-iz) disappears suddenly from sight

zany (ZAY-nee) funny in a strange way

Index

Read More

Claybourne, Anna. *Don't Read This Book Before Bed: Thrills, Chills, and Hauntingly True Stories.* Washington, DC: National Geographic (2017).

Rudolph, Jessica. *Creaky Castles (Tiptoe Into Scary Places).* New York: Bearport (2017).

Learn More Online

To learn more about lurid London, visit:
www.bearportpublishing.com/Tiptoe

About the Author

E. Merwin is an author who enjoys researching haunted histories. As for the ghosts, she wishes them well in this world—and in the next.